Dear Adam,
enjoy the story and
maybe you can learn
a little German ... :)

Have a wonderful time
and be good!

Love + hugs

The Robber Hotzenplotz

OTFRIED PREUßLER

Translated by Anthea Bell
Illustrated by F.J. Tripp

THIENEMANN

The Man with Seven Knives

One day Kasperl's grandmother was sitting in the sun outside her house, **grinding** coffee. Kasperl and his friend Seppel had given her a new coffee mill for her birthday. It was a musical coffee mill; they had invented it themselves. When Grandmother turned the **handle**, it played "Nuts in May". "Nuts in May" was the tune Grandmother liked best.

Now that Grandmother had her new coffee mill she enjoyed grinding coffee beans so much that she drank twice as much coffee as before. For the second time that day she had filled up the mill with coffee beans. She was just going to turn the handle again when suddenly she heard a **rustling, snapping** noise in the bushes.

"Hand that thing over!", said a rough voice.

Grandmother looked up in surprise. She settled her glasses on her nose.

A strange man was standing beside her. He had a bushy black beard and a terrible hooked nose. He wore a **slouched hat** with a **crooked** feather in it, and he held a pistol in his right hand. With his left hand he pointed at Grandmother's coffee mill.

"Hand it over, I tell you."

But Grandmother was not afraid.

"I beg your pardon!", she said **indignantly**. "How did you get in – and what do you mean by shouting at me like that? Who are you, anyway?"

The stranger laughed so much that the feather in his hat wagged **to and fro**.

"Don't you read the papers, Grandmother? I'll give you three guesses."

For the first time Grandmother noticed that the man had a sword and seven knives stuck in his broad leather belt. She turned pale.

"Are you – would you **by any chance** be the robber Hotzen-plotz?", she asked, her voice trembling.

"That's me!", said the man with the seven knives. "Don't make a song and dance about it. I don't like **fuss**. Give me that coffee mill at once."

"But it doesn't belong to you."

"**Fiddlesticks!**", said the robber Hotzenplotz. "Just do as I tell you. I'm going to count three ..."

And he raised his pistol.

"Please don't!", said Grandmother. "You can't take my coffee mill. I had it for my birthday. When I turn the handle it plays a lovely tune."

"Exactly!", growled the robber Hotzenplotz. "*I* would like a musical coffee mill, too. Hand it over, now."

Grandmother **heaved** a deep sigh and gave him the coffee mill. What else could she do?

Every day the newspapers were full of stories about the wicked robber Hotzenplotz. All the people were terrified of him, even Sergeant Dimplemoser – and Sergeant Dimplemoser was a policeman.

"There now, that's better!"

With a grunt of satisfaction, Hotzenplotz **stowed** Grandmother's coffee mill away in his **knapsack**. Then he closed his left eye. He glared at Grandmother with his right eye.

"Now, you listen to me", he said. "You're to stay sitting on the bench here. Don't move an inch. Sit and count nine hundred and ninety-nine **under your breath**."

"What for?", asked Grandmother.

"I'll tell you what for", replied Hotzenplotz. "When you've finished counting nine hundred and ninety-nine you can call for help. I don't mind. But not a moment sooner, do you hear me? Or you'll be sorry for it. All right?"

"All right", whispered Grandmother.

"And no cheating."

As a **parting** gesture the robber Hotzenplotz waved his pistol at her again. Then he swung himself over the garden fence and disappeared.

Kasperl's grandmother sat on the seat outside her cottage, white as a sheet and trembling. The robber was gone, and so was her coffee mill.

It was a long time before Grandmother could begin counting.

Obediently she counted nine hundred and ninety-nine.

One, two, three, four ... not too fast, not too slow.

But she was so upset that she kept counting wrong. She had to go back to the beginning at least a dozen times.

At last she got to nine hundred and ninety-nine.

She cried "Help!" in a **piercing** voice.

Then she fell down in a faint

to grind: mahlen – handle: Griff – to rustle: rascheln – to snap: schnipsen, knacken – slouched hat: Schlapphut – crooked: krumm – indignant: entrüstet – to and fro: hin und her – by any chance: wohl, etwa – fuss: Theater, Getue – fiddlesticks: Quatsch, Papperlapapp – to heave: ausstoßen – to stow: verstauen – knapsack: Proviantbeutel, Schnappsack – under one's breath: für sich selbst, leise – to part: sich trennen, verabschieden – obedient: gehorsam – piercing: gellend – to fall in a faint: in Ohnmacht fallen

A Helping Hand for the Police

Kasperl and his friend Seppel were out shopping. They had been to the baker's to buy a bag of flour, some **yeast**, and two pounds of sugar. Next they were going to the **dairy** to buy some cream. It was Sunday tomorrow, and on Sunday Grandmother always had plum pie and **whipped cream**. Kasperl and Seppel looked forward to that plum pie all week.

"Do you know what?", said Kasperl. "I'd like to be **Emperor** of Constantinople."

"What for?", asked Seppel.

"Because then I could eat plum pie and whipped cream every day."

"Does the Emperor of Constantinople have plum pie and whipped cream every day?"

Kasperl **shrugged** his shoulders.

"I don't know. But that's what I'd do if *I* were Emperor of Constantinople."

"So would I!", sighed Seppel.

"So would you?", inquired Kasperl. "Oh no, that wouldn't work!"

"Why not?"

"Because there's only one Emperor of Constantinople, not two. So if I'm Emperor of Constantinople, you can't be Emperor of Constantinople too. You must see that!"

"Mmph", said Seppel. "We'd just have to **take turns** then. One week you, and the next week me!"

"Not a bad idea", Kasperl agreed. "Not bad at all."

All of a sudden they heard a distant cry for help.

"Listen!", said Seppel in alarm. "Wasn't that Grand-mother?"

"Yes, it *was* Grandmother!", said Kasperl. "I wonder what the matter is."

"I don't know", said Seppel. "Maybe there's something wrong ..."

"Quick, let's go and see!"

Kasperl and Seppel turned round and ran home. As they reached Grandmother's garden gate they nearly ran into Sergeant Dimplemoser.

He, too, had heard someone calling for help, so he came hurrying along.

"Can't you look where you're going?", he said **crossly**. "You're **obstructing** me in the execution of my duty. It's against the law."

He strode into the garden after Kasperl and Seppel. They found Grandmother flat on her back on the **lawn** by the garden seat. She was lying perfectly still.

"Is it very bad?", asked Seppel, hiding his eyes.

"No", said Kasperl. "I think she's only fainted."

They carried Grandmother carefully into the sitting-room and put her down on the sofa.

Kasperl sprinkled her hands and face with cold water. The water **revived** her.

"Just think what's happened!", said Grandmother.

"What *has* happened?", asked Kasperl and Seppel.

"I've been robbed!"

"You don't say so!", interrupted Sergeant Dimplemoser. "Robbed, were you? Who by?"

"It was the robber Hotzenplotz."

"Wait a minute. This is **evidence**. I must take it down."

The sergeant busily opened his notebook and pulled out a pencil.

"Begin at the beginning, Grandmother. Tell the truth, the whole truth, and nothing but the truth, and speak clearly and not too fast, so that I can write it all down. As for you two –", he turned to Kasperl and Seppel, "you just keep quiet until we've done with the evidence. Remember I'm an officer of the law. Is that clear?"

So Grandmother told the whole story. Sergeant Dimplemoser wrote it down in his notebook, looking very important.

"Shall I get my beautiful new coffee mill back now?", asked Grandmother, when he had finally finished writing and shut his notebook.

"Of course", said the sergeant.

"How long will it take?"

"Well – that depends. Of course, we have to catch the robber Hotzenplotz first. Unfortunately, we don't even know where he hides out yet. He's a **sly** one. He's been **running circles round the police** for two and a half years now. But we'll get him one of these days, never fear! We place the **utmost reliance** upon the **zealous** co-operation of the public."

"You place what where?", asked Kasperl.

Sergeant Dimplemoser **quelled** him with a glance.

"Are you deaf, Kasperl?", he asked. "We place the *utmost reliance* upon the *zealous co-operation* of the *public*!"

"What does it mean?"

"It means that people must help us get on the thief's **trail**."

"Oh!", said Kasperl. "Would it help if anyone actually caught the thief?"

"Well, of course, that would be best of all", agreed Sergeant

Dimplemoser, stroking his **moustache**. "But who do you think is going to try anything as dangerous as that?"

"We are!", said Kasperl. "Seppel and me – are you coming too, Seppel?"

"Of course I am", said Seppel. "We have to help the police. We'll catch the robber Hotzenplotz."

But catching robbers is not as easy as all that

yeast: Hefe – **dairy:** Milchladen – **whipped cream:** Schlagsahne – **Emperor:** Kaiser – **to shrug:** zucken – **to take turns:** sich abwechseln – **all of a sudden:** plötzlich – **cross:** böse, wütend – **to obstruct:** behindern – **lawn:** Rasen, Gras – **to revive:** beleben, wieder zu sich kommen – **evidence:** Zeugenaussage – **sly:** gerissen – **to run circles round s.o.:** jmd. an der Nase herumführen – **utmost reliance:** größtes Vertrauen – **zealous:** eifrig, rege – **to quell:** bezwingen, tadeln – **trail:** Spur – **moustache:** Schnurrbart

Grandmother was rather worried, but Kasperl and Seppel **stuck to their guns.** They were going to catch the robber Hotzenplotz and get Grandmother's coffee mill back. The only **drawback** was that they didn't know where to find the robber's **den.**

"We'll soon find out!", said Kasperl. They spent Sunday morning thinking. Then all of a sudden Kasperl began to laugh.

"What's the joke?", asked Seppel.

"Well, now I know what to do."

"What?"

"You'll soon see."

Kasperl and Seppel found an empty **crate** in Grandmother's cellar. It had once held potatoes. They carried it into the garden. Then they **shovelled** fine white sand into it.

"Now what?"

"Now we'll put the **lid** on."

They put the lid on the crate, and Kasperl fetched a dozen nails and a hammer.

"There – nail it down, Seppel. As hard as you can."

Seppel nodded and set to work. With the very first stroke of the hammer he hit his thumb. How it hurt! However, he **clenched his teeth** and went on hammering bravely, like an expert nailer-down-of-potato-crate-lids.

Meanwhile, Kasperl was getting the big paintbrush from the **attic** and mixing a pot of red paint. When he came back with the paintpot and the brush, Seppel had just hit his thumb for the fiftyseventh time. But the lid was firmly nailed down.

"Now, watch this!", said Kasperl.

He loaded the brush with red paint, and, much to Seppel's astonishment, wrote on the potato crate, in huge bright letters:

Caution
Gold !!

What could it mean? Seppel **racked his brains**, but he couldn't **make head or tail of it**.

"Do you know what?", said Kasperl. "You could be making yourself useful by fetching the **handcart** from the shed, **instead of** just standing there sucking your thumb."

Seppel went off to the shed and wheeled out the handcart. Then he had to help Kasperl lift the crate. It was hard work; they were puffing and blowing like **grampuses**.

"Oh dear!", groaned Seppel. "And on a Sunday, too!"

As if things weren't bad enough already! There was no plum pie and whipped cream in Grandmother's house today – Grandmother was too sad about her coffee mill to make plum pie. Now they had to work like slaves too.

In the end they did it.

"Now what?", asked Seppel.

"Now for the important part."

Kasperl took a **gimlet** out of his pocket and bored a little hole in the bottom of the crate. When he removed the gimlet, sand trickled out of the hole.

"There", said Kasperl with satisfaction. "**That should do the trick.**"

Then he sharpened a **matchstick** with his penknife and stopped up the hole he had just bored.

Seppel had been watching, shaking his head **in bewilderment**.

"I'm sorry", he said, "but I just don't see the point of that."

"Don't you?", said Kasperl, laughing. "It's quite simple. Tomorrow morning the two of us will wheel the crate out into the woods on the handcart. Hotzenplotz will be lying **in wait**. When he sees us coming he'll read the words on our crate and he'll think there's gold inside."

"Oho", said Seppel. "Then what?"

"Well, then he'll want to have the crate, of course. We'll let him jump out at us, and then we'll run away. Hotzenplotz will **pounce on** the crate and take it – well ... where do you think he'll take it?"

"How should I know, Kasperl? I'm not the robber Hotzen-plotz."

"Why, it's easy, Seppel! He'll take it to his den. But on the way the sand will be trickling out of the hole in the crate. So there'll be a little trail of sand going through the wood. If we want to find the robber's den we only have to follow the trail and it will lead us straight to him. What do you think of that?"

"Wonderful", said Seppel. "What a good idea. But don't forget to take out the matchstick before we run away."

"Don't worry!", said Kasperl. "I shall remember all right."

And he made a big knot in his **handkerchief**.

A knot in your handkerchief is often very useful

to stick to one's guns: bei seinem Entschluss bleiben – **drawback**: Nachteil, Problem – **den**: Versteck – **crate**: Kiste – **to shovel**: schaufeln – **lid**: Deckel – **to clench one's teeth**: die Zähne zusammenbeißen – **attic**: Dachboden, Speicher – **to rack one's brains**: den Kopf zerbrechen – **to make head or tail of it**: aus etwas schlau werden, verstehen – **handcart**: Handwagen – **instead of**: anstatt – **grampus**: Delphin – **gimlet**: Bohrer – **that should do the trick**: das müsste klappen – **matchstick**: Streichholz – **in bewilderment**: verwundert – **in wait**: auf der Lauer – **to pounce on sth.**: sich auf etwas stürzen – **handkerchief**: Taschentuch

A Piece of
Bad Luck

The robber Hotzenplotz worked very hard at his job. During the summer he got up **at six o'clock sharp** every morning. He left his cave at half past seven, at the latest, and went off to work. This particular morning he was lying in wait behind the **gorse** bushes on the **outskirts** of the wood. He had been there since eight o'clock, watching the road through his telescope. Now it was half past nine and still there was no one to be robbed.

"Times are bad!", grumbled the robber Hotzenplotz. "If things go on like this I'll have to look around for another job, that's what it will come to. Robbery **doesn't pay much** in the long run, and it's hard work too."

He was just going to take **a pinch of snuff** (though he seldom allowed himself to take snuff in working hours) when he heard a handcart **creaking** along the road.

"Oho!", thought Hotzenplotz. "I've not been wasting my time after all." Instead of reaching for his snuff box he raised his telescope again.

On the road, two people and a handcart were just coming around the corner. There was a big crate on the cart. It looked heavy. The two people were having hard work to push the cart along.

What's more, one of them was Kasperl! It was easy to **tell** him by his **pointed cap**.

Who was the other one?

Well, if one of them was Kasperl, then the other could only
be his friend Seppel. Even the robber Hotzenplotz knew that.

"I do wish I knew what was in that crate!", he thought.

But wait – wasn't there a notice on the crate? What did
those bright red letters say ...?

"Caution – Gold!", read the robber Hotzenplotz. He read it a second time and then a third time to make sure he had it right.

No, there was no mistake. He had **struck lucky** at last. Perhaps he needn't change his job after all.

Swiftly Hotzenplotz pulled the pistol out of his belt and **cocked** it. He let Kasperl, Seppel and the cart come within a few feet of him. Then he took a great **leap** and jumped out into the road.

"Hands up", bellowed Hotzenplotz, "or I fire!"

He was not in the least surprised when Kasperl and Seppel **took to their heels.**

"Run, you two heroes, run!", he shouted after them. "So long as the crate doesn't run after you! Ha, ha, ha!"

He **roared with laughter**, put the pistol back in his belt and settled down to take a closer look at the crate.

"Hm – nailed down! Of course, it would be – after all, there's gold inside. Shall I just open it and **have a peep**? Better not ... I must get out of here. Kasperl and Seppel will have gone for the police. Not that I'm afraid of the police! I am the robber Hotzenplotz, I'm not afraid! Still, better safe than sorry."

Hotzenplotz wasted no time in **hoisting** the heavy crate up on his back. The handcart would be of no use on the path through the woods. He kicked it into the **ditch**. Puffing and blowing, he carried his **booty** home through the woods to his cave.

He was in such a hurry to get home that he never noticed

that the crate on his back was growing lighter and lighter as he went along. For at the very last moment Kasperl had remembered to take out the matchstick. All the time fine white sand was trickling through the hole at the bottom of the crate. The robber Hotzenplotz left a trail behind him.

When he got home, Hotzenplotz put the crate down on the table. He **bolted** the door of his cave, took the hammer and **pliers** out of his tool box, and set to work opening the crate. He was an experienced robber who knew his job **inside out**, so it was not long before he had the lid open.

He bent over the crate and looked inside. Then he froze.

He couldn't believe his eyes. There was nothing but a little heap of sand in the crate – perfectly ordinary white sand.

"Ha!", cried the robber Hotzenplotz in a rage. "I've been **cheated**! I've been **fooled**!"

He grabbed his curved sword in both hands, fell upon the poor potato crate and chopped it into little bits. He chopped the **stout** oak table into little bits too. Then he ran out of doors to get some fresh air.

What did he see?

There was a fine trail of sand on the ground ... It led from the woods right up to his cave. Hotzenplotz didn't have to think very hard to realize what that meant.

He let fly a terrible **oath**.

"Kasperl and Seppel meant to trick me, did they?", snarled the robber Hotzenplotz. "I'll **turn the tables** on them now! Just let them wait, the precious pair of them! **Revenge**, revenge!"

at six o'clock sharp: pünktlich um sechs Uhr – gorse: Ginster – outskirts: Rand – doesn't pay much: sich nicht lohnen – a pinch of snuff: eine Prise Schnupftabak – to creak: knarren – to tell: erkennen – pointed cap: Zipfelmütze – to strike lucky: Glück haben – to cock: spannen – leap: Sprung, Satz – to take to one's heels: sich aus dem Staub machen, Reißaus nehmen – to roar with laughter: in schallendes Gelächter ausbrechen – to have a peep: (kurz) hineinschauen – to hoist: aufladen, hochheben – ditch: Straßengraben – booty: Beute – to bolt: verriegeln – pliers: Zange – inside out: in- und auswendig, von Grund auf – to cheat: betrügen – to fool: zum Narren halten – stout: stark – oath: Fluch – to turn the tables: den Spieß umdrehen – revenge: Rache

Kasperl and Seppel had not run for the police, only around the corner. There they slipped into the bushes and waited. They were delighted when they saw Hotzenplotz dragging the potato crate off.

"I feel quite sorry for him, poor man", said Seppel.

"Whatever for?", asked Kasperl.

"He's got to carry that heavy crate so far, all by himself. I hope he doesn't get flat feet."

"Him?", muttered Kasperl. "He can carry it **blue in the face,** for all I care! Don't forget he's a robber. He stole Grandmother's coffee mill!"

They stayed hiding around the corner a little longer, just to make sure. Then they crept back to the place where Hotzenplotz had jumped out at them. The empty handcart was lying upside down in the ditch.

"It's all right", said Kasperl. "We'll leave it there till we come back."

And now for the trail of sand! They did not have to search for it long. There was the trail, leading into the woods.

Kasperl wanted to hurry off at once, but Seppel held him back. "Wait a minute!", he said. "We must **disguise** ourselves first."

"Disguise ourselves?"

"Yes, of course! We don't want the robber Hotzenplotz to recognize us, do we?"

"Mm – you're right. But how can we get hold of disguises here?"

"Easy! I'll lend you my hat, and you can give me your pointed cap."

"And what am I supposed to do with your hat?", asked Kasperl.

"What a silly question!", said Seppel. "Put it on! Does it fit?"

"No, it doesn't", said Kasperl.

Seppel's hat was far too big for him. It made him look like a **scarecrow** out for the day. But Seppel thought it looked perfect.

"Splendid!", he said. "No one would ever know you! How do I look in your cap?"

"Very funny", said Kasperl. "If Grandmother could see you she'd fall down in another faint."

"Then that's all right. The robber Hotzenplotz will never know us now. Come on, let's go."

But robbers are not always as stupid
as you might think

Kasperl and Seppel followed the fine trail of sand which Hotzenplotz had left behind. The trail was quite clear, but as they went on the woods became thicker and darker.

"Ugh!", thought Seppel. "This really is a wood for robbers. What a good thing we're heavily disguised!"

They had been walking for about an hour when Kasperl, who was in front, suddenly stopped.

"What's the matter?", asked Seppel.

The trail on the ground had divided. They could hardly believe their eyes. Instead of one trail, suddenly there were two. One trail led to the right, the other to the left.

"Can you **make** it **out**, Seppel?", asked Kasperl.

"Yes, Kasperl. One of them must be a false trail."

"I'm afraid that must be it. But which of them is the real trail?"

"I don't know. We must find out. We'd better go different ways."

"All right, Seppel. Will you go right or left?"

"Let's **toss** for it."

"All right."

Kasperl and Seppel tossed a coin. Seppel threw heads twice and tails once. That meant he was to go left.

"Good luck – and be careful, Seppel."

"Yes, Kasperl", said Seppel. "I'll be very careful. Good luck to you too!"

blue in the face: bis er schwarz wird – to disguise: sich verkleiden – scarecrow: Vogelscheuche – to make out: verstehen – to toss: Münze werfen, losen

A Pistol Full of Pepper

The robber Hotzenplotz grinned and stroked his bushy black beard. He was glad he had thought of using the sand that was left in the crate to make a second trail. He hoped Kasperl and Seppel would be silly enough to **separate**. At the end of the trail each of them was going to get the surprise of his life. Hotzenplotz **had seen to** that!

The left-hand trail led to the robber's cave. The **catch** was that the robber Hotzenplotz was waiting behind the trunk of a **gnarled** old oak tree not far from the cave door, with his pistol cocked. In fact there were no bullets in his pistol, but it was loaded with **ground** pepper. A pistol full of pepper was the way to deal with Kasperl and Seppel, thought the robber Hotzenplotz.

"Are those **lads** going to keep me waiting much longer?", Hotzenplotz wondered. No – unless he was much mistaken, here came someone **groping** his way through the woods.

Sure enough, someone came into sight through the trees! He was wearing a bright red pointed cap. So it was Kasperl!

Hotzenplotz was not to know that Seppel had Kasperl's cap. **Callously** he raised his pistol full of pepper and **took aim**.

He aimed very carefully, crooking his finger slowly ... Crash! There was a flash and a bang and a little cloud of pepper.

Poor Seppel! The pepper struck him right in the face. He couldn't see or hear; he was sneezing and coughing and choking without a moment's relief. How it burned and prickled and stung his eyes! It was horrible!

The robber Hotzenplotz made short work of him.

Jeering, he bound Seppel's hands and feet with a rope, **flung** him over his shoulder and bore him off to the cave. He threw him down in a corner.

"There!", he cried. "Sneeze away then! Bless you!"

He waited until Seppel had **recovered** a little. When he saw that the pepper was **wearing off**, he gave Seppel a kick.

"How are you this fine day, Kasperl?", he jeered. "Welcome to my cave! Do you like it here? I'm so sorry you seem to have a **cold**. But that's what comes of **meddling** in other people's business."

Seppel couldn't answer. Seppel sneezed.

"Bless you, Kasperl!", said the robber Hotzenplotz again.

Did he say Kasperl?

"I'm not Kasperl!", said Seppel. He fell to sneezing again.

"Oh no!" Hotzenplotz grinned. "Of course, you're not Kasperl at all, you're the Emperor of Constantinople."

"No, I'm not. I'm Seppel."

"To be sure you are – and I'm Sergeant Dimplemoser, in case you didn't know."

34

"But I really am Seppel!"

"**Hold your tongue!**", growled the robber Hotzenplotz. "If you **tell** me **stories** I shall get cross and beat you with the **poker**. Aha – listen to that ..."

Ting-a-ling-a-ling-a-ling.

A little bell hanging on the door **post** of the cave was ringing.

"Do you know what that means?", asked the robber Hotzenplotz. "No, you wouldn't know. Let me tell you. That bell means that your friend Seppel has just **tumbled down** a hole – into a **trap** I set for him. That's quite a surprise, isn't it? **Lost your tongue**, have you? But never mind, better brains than yours have failed to **get the best of** Hotzenplotz!"

The robber roared with laughter and **slapped his thigh**. Then he pulled some rope and a sack out from under the bed.

"Now I'm going to fetch your friend Seppel to **keep** you **company**," he said. "While I'm out, think it over and see if you aren't Kasperl after all. Have a good time!"

---

to separate: sich trennen – **to see to sth.**: dafür sorgen – **catch**: Haken, Problem – **gnarled**: knorrig – **ground**: gemahlen – **lad**: Bursche – **to grope**: suchen, herumtappen – **callous**: herzlos, kaltblütig – **to take aim**: zielen – **jeering**: höhnisch – **to fling**: werfen – **to recover**: sich erholen – **to wear off**: nachlassen, sich verlieren – **cold**: Schnupfen – **to meddle in**: sich einmischen – **to hold one's tongue**: den Mund halten – **to tell stories**: anschwindeln – **poker**: Schürhaken – **post**: Pfosten – **to tumble down**: hineinfallen – **trap**: Falle – **to lose one's tongue**: sprachlos sein – **to get the best of**: fertig werden mit – **to slap one's thigh**: sich auf die Schenkel klopfen – **to keep company**: Gesellschaft leisten

A Gloomy Outlook

Meanwhile, what about Kasperl?

After parting from Seppel, Kasperl followed "his" trail far into the woods. He grumbled to himself as he went along. He was **cross with** the robber Hotzenplotz, he was cross with the miserable path full of **roots** and **brambles** which led to the robber's den, and last but not least he was cross with Seppel's hat.

Seppel's hat would keep falling down over his face. He kept pushing it back on his head, but before he had gone another step or so further it was sure to be sitting on his nose again.

"It might be better the other way around", thought Kasperl, putting the hat on back to front.

However, that was no good.

Time after time Kasperl had to push the stupid hat back on his head. Time after time Seppel's green hat slipped down over

his face again – until all of a sudden there was a loud crack-
ing, crashing noise. Still wearing Seppel's hat, Kasperl tumbled down a hole. There were traps hidden by branches all
around the robber's cave.

So there was poor Kasperl, one floor lower. It was not what
he had expected. He rubbed his **seat** tenderly. Lucky he had-
n't broken any bones! He might easily have broken something, falling so far and landing so hard.

"How stupid!", thought Kasperl, looking at the **pit**. "Four
smooth walls going straight up and that's all. How am I ever
going to get out?"

But there was still Seppel. Seppel would be sure to find him
and get him out. After all, Seppel was his best friend.

Would he **turn up** before long? Kasperl **pricked up his ears**.
He thought he heard someone coming. Unfortunately, someone was not his friend Seppel, but the robber Hotzenplotz. It
was a nasty shock for Kasperl when the robber's face with its
bushy black beard peered over the edge of the pit.

"Hello there, Seppel!", shouted Hotzenplotz. "You haven't
broken your neck, I hope? Aren't you going to say hello to
kind uncle? Just think, Uncle Hotzenplotz has come to help
you out! I suppose you *do* want to get out?"

Kasperl **nodded**. Of course he wanted to get out. Once he
was out of the trap the rest could take care of itself. He might
get a chance to run away.

"Listen!", said Hotzenplotz. "Do exactly what I tell you.
I'm going to let down a sack on this rope – like this, you
see ... Now, get in the sack, Seppel!"

"In the sack?", asked Kasperl, **hesitating**.

"That's right, get in the sack", said Hotzenplotz. "I'm going to **haul** you **up** in it. That's the only way you'll get out. Hurry up, do! And don't leave your hat down there!"

To be sure – Seppel's hat!

Kasperl picked it up off the ground and put it on his head. Then he climbed into the sack, and the robber Hotzenplotz pulled him out of the hole. It was like going up in a lift. But once the robber had him safely out, he did exactly what Kasperl himself would have done in his place. He **tied up** the sack. Now Kasperl was well and truly caught.

He struggled and shouted, but it was no good. Hotzenplotz flung the sack over his shoulder, and off they went to the robber's cave.

"Well, here we are!"

Hotzenplotz dumped the sack on the floor beside Seppel.

"Now we'll see who's Seppel and who's Kasperl!", he said.

He opened the sack a little, just enough for Kasperl to put his head out. It was wearing Seppel's hat. The robber Hotzenplotz would not let him out any farther.

"*Now* will you **admit** that you're Kasperl?", he **gnarled** at Seppel.

Seppel was just going to repeat "No, I'm not. I'm Seppel". But Kasperl got in first. He winked at Seppel. It might be quite useful if the robber mixed them up ...

"Why don't you answer me, fellow?"

"What do you expect him to say?", said Kasperl, answering instead of Seppel. "You know best, Mr. Plotzenhotz!"

"Plotzenhotz! My name is Hotzenplotz!"

"I'm so sorry, Mr. Lotzenpotz."

"Stupid!"

"Who – me?", said Kasperl.

"My name is Hotzenplotz, do you hear? Can't you remember even the simplest name?"

"Why, of course I can, Mr. Potzenlotz!"

Hotzenplotz took a pinch of snuff.

He saw that it was no use **getting annoyed**. Obviously this Seppel really was as stupid as his green hat made him look.

The robber carefully unfolded a big checked handkerchief. He sneezed and blew his nose.

When he had finished blowing his nose he put the handkerchief away, went over to Kasperl and Seppel, hooked his **thumbs** into his belt, and **addressed** them.

"You were going to spy on me. Now you're in my power", said Hotzenplotz. "That's how it is. You **deserve no pity**. I could **make mincemeat of** you if I wanted to. But it doesn't happen to **suit** me. And why not?" He took another pinch of snuff and sneezed before going on.

"Because I've thought of something better to do with you, that's why. You, Kasperl –", he pointed to Seppel, "I'm going to chain you up. You will stay in the cave and work for me **until you're black in the face**. As for you, Seppel –", Hotzenplotz pointed to Kasperl, "I'm going to sell you!"

"Oh goodness me!", groaned Kasperl. "Who to?"

"Who to?", said Hotzenplotz. "To my old friend the wicked **magician** Petrosilius Zackleman!"

---

to be cross with s.b.: auf jmd. sauer sein – **root**: Wurzel – **bramble**: Dornenranke – **seat**: Hinterteil – **pit**: Grube – **to turn up**: auftauchen – **to prick up one's ears**: die Ohren spitzen – **to nod**: nicken – **to hesitate**: zögern – **to haul up**: hinaufziehen – **to tie up**: zubinden – **to admit**: zugeben – **to gnarl**: knurren – **to get annoyed**: ärgerlich werden – **thumb**: Daumen – **to address s.b.**: jmd. ansprechen, sich jmd. zuwenden – **to deserve no pity**: kein Mitleid verdienen – **to make mincemeat of s.b.**: Hackfleisch aus jmd. machen – **to suit**: in den Kram passen – **until you're black in the face**: bis du schwarz wirst – **magician**: Zauberer

Petrosilius Zackleman

The **wicked** magician Petrosilius Zackleman was sitting in the kitchen of his **enchanted castle**, peeling potatoes and feeling cross.

Petrosilius Zackleman was a great magician. He could easily turn people into animals or birds. He could turn **mud** into gold. But hard as he had tried, he had never managed to **cast a spell** for peeling potatoes by magic. So unless he wanted to **be stuck with** nothing but noodles and rice, he was forced to put on an **apron**, from time to time, and get down to the **dreary** job of peeling potatoes himself.

"All because I haven't got a **servant**!", sighed the great magician Petrosilius Zackleman.

And why hadn't he got a servant?

"Because I've never been able to find the right one", he thought. "The right servant for me must be stupid, that's the main thing. I couldn't have a clever person in my enchanted castle, or he might find out my secrets. Magicians have to be so careful. I'd rather peel my own potatoes than make that kind of trouble for myself – though it *is* annoying."

Petrosilius Zackleman had stopped working while he thought about his troubles. He was just going to start peeling potatoes again when the doorbell rang.

"Wait a moment!", cried the great magician Petrosilius Zackleman. "I'm coming."

He ran into the hall and took hold of the heavy bolt. He was about to open the great gate of the castle, but at the last moment he realized he was still wearing the apron.

Good gracious!

Petrosilius Zackleman in an apron! Suppose anyone saw him in such an **undignified** costume!

The doorbell rang again.

"All right, I'm coming!", cried Zackleman.

He tore off the apron – but where could he put it down?

"Abracadabra!"

The great magician Petrosilius Zackleman snapped his fingers. The apron flew back to the kitchen all by itself and hung itself up on its hook in the **china** cupboard.

The bell rang for the third time.

Petrosilius Zackleman pushed back the bolt and opened the gate. Outside stood the robber Hotzenplotz with a sack on his back.

"Well, look who's here!", cried the great magician with pleasure. "How are you, old friend? Welcome to my castle! Won't you come in?"

"Delighted", said Hotzenplotz.

Petrosilius Zackleman led him into the **study**. This was a **great treat** for Hotzenplotz. The great magician took only his best friends into the study. Ordinary visitors were received in the great hall of the castle – if they were received at all, that is.

Zackleman's study held an enormous bookcase full of thick **leather-bound** books. The desk, the **window sill** and the floor were covered with piles of more thick leather-bound books. Over the desk was a crocodile hanging from the **ceiling** (it was a **stuffed** crocodile). A skeleton stood in the corner holding a lighted candle in its **bony** right hand.

Petrosilius Zackleman sat down in his chair behind the desk, and pointed to an armchair opposite.

"Won't you sit down, old fellow?"

Hotzenplotz nodded and sat down.

"A pinch of snuff?", asked the great magician.

"**Try me!**"

Zackleman snapped his fingers and put his hand out into empty air. A silver snuff box suddenly appeared by magic. He offered it to Hotzenplotz.

"Help yourself!"

Hotzenplotz took a huge pinch of snuff. He sneezed so hard that the crocodile almost fell down from the ceiling.

"Thunder and lightning, I call that snuff, old friend!", he exclaimed. "It's three times stronger than pepper! Where do you get it?"

"My own make", said the great magician. "My special blend. It's called 'Nosecomfort'. Here, have another!"

Hotzenplotz **beamed** with delight. He had an idea. He took a pinch of snuff and sneezed. Then he said: "Couldn't we do a **deal**?"

"A deal?", asked Zackleman.

"Yes", said Hotzenplotz, "with your snuff."

Zackleman wrinkled up his nose.

"What can you offer me?", he asked. "Don't you know I'm **rolling in riches?**"

"Who said anything about money?", inquired Hotzenplotz. "I can offer you something much better than money. Guess!"

Petrosilius Zackleman frowned heavily and thought hard.

Hotzenplotz waited for a few minutes. Then he said: "Shall I give you a hint? It's something you've been wanting for a long time. Something you just couldn't find."

"Something I've been wanting for a long time. Something I just couldn't find." The great magician pricked up his ears. "Is it – could it be a new book of magic?"

"No, it's a servant!"

"What?", cried the great magician Petrosilius Zackleman. "Really? A servant! But is he stupid enough?"

"As stupid **as they come**", said the robber Hotzenplotz.

"And where have you got him?"

"In this sack here."

Hotzenplotz **undid** the string of the sack. The sack fell to the ground. Kasperl popped out with Seppel's hat on his head.

Petrosilius Zackleman snapped his fingers. His glasses appeared by magic.

He put them on his nose and looked Kasperl up and down. Kasperl looked as stupid as he could.

"Is he as stupid as he looks?", asked the great magician Petrosilius Zackleman.

"Every bit as stupid", said Hotzenplotz.

"Good", said Zackleman. "*Very* good. What's his name?"

"Seppel."

"Aha. Well, Seppel, you're **hired**. Can you peel potatoes?"

"Of course, Mr. Saggleman", said Kasperl.

Petrosilius Zackleman **flew into a temper**.

"Say my name wrong, would you?", he cried furiously. "What's more, I'm not just Mister. You are to call me 'Great Magician Petrosilius Zackleman'. Remember that!"

"Very well, Great Magician Zeprodilius Woggleswan", said Kasperl innocently.

"Thunder and lightning!"

The great magician seized Kasperl by the **collar** and shook him back and forth.

"Do you think I'm going to let you make fun of me? Do you want me to turn you into a monkey **on the spot**? Or a worm?"

Petrosilius Zackleman snapped his fingers – and **lo and**

behold! His **magic staff** flew to his hand! But the robber Hotzenplotz did not want him to cast a spell on Kasperl. He caught Zackleman's arm and **soothed** him **down**.

"Seppel isn't getting your name wrong **on purpose**, old friend", he explained. "He just can't remember it. He's too stupid."

"Is that so?", said Petrosilius Zackleman. Then he laughed. "Hotzenplotz!", he cried. "I can't tell you how happy I am. I'm delighted with this Seppel of yours. He might have been made for me! I'll take him straight to the kitchen; he can start peeling potatoes. Then you and I will fix the price **at our leisure**."

"I'd rather fix it now", said the robber Hotzenplotz.

"All right. I'll give you – shall we say, half a sack of snuff?"

"Half a sack?", replied Hotzenplotz. "That's not much for a whole servant."

"Very well", said Petrosilius Zackleman. "You can have a whole sack. Done?"

a - tishoo !

He offered Hotzenplotz his hand.

"Done!", said Hotzenplotz, shaking hands. "Seppel's yours – now you can do whatever you like with him."

wicked: böse – **enchanted castle**: Zauberschloss – **mud**: Dreck – **to cast a spell**: zaubern, verzaubern – **to be stuck with**: dasitzen mit – **apron**: Küchenschürze – **dreary**: langweilig, lästig – **servant**: Dienstbote – **good gracious!**: Ach du liebe Zeit! – **undignified**: unwürdig – **china**: Geschirr – **study**: Studierzimmer – **great treat**: hohe Ehre – **leather-bound**: in Leder eingebunden – **window sill**: Fensterbank – **ceiling**: Decke – **stuffed**: ausgestopft – **bony**: knöchern – **try me!**: Lass mich probieren, immer her damit! – **to beam**: strahlen – **deal**: Geschäft – **to roll in riches**: in Geld schwimmen – **as they come**: wie's nur geht – **to undo**: aufmachen – **to hire**: einstellen – **to fly into a temper**: einen Wutanfall bekommen – **collar**: Kragen – **on the spot**: auf der Stelle – **lo and behold!**: Und siehe da! – **magic staff**: Zauberstab – **to soothe s.b. down**: jmd. beschwichtigen – **on purpose**: absichtlich – **at one's leisure**: in aller Ruhe – **a-tishoo!**: Hatschi!

48

An Adventure in the Dark

Kasperl spent the rest of the day peeling potatoes in the kitchen of Zackleman's castle. The wicked magician just couldn't have too many of those potatoes – the first potatoes he had not had to peel for himself. At dinner time he **devoured** seven **helpings** of mashed potatoes, and for supper he ate six and a half dozen potato cakes with onion sauce. No wonder he was in a very good mood that evening.

At last he got up from the table and clapped Kasperl on the shoulder in a friendly way.

"That will do for today", he said. "Now I'll show you where you sleep. Follow me, Seppel!"

Kasperl followed the great magician Petrosilius Zackleman across the hall into a small room. The room held an empty **bedstead** and a **washstand**.

"This is your bedroom, Seppel", said the magician. "You will sleep here."

"Here? On the empty bedstead?", asked Kasperl.

"Just wait a minute!", said Petrosilius Zackleman.

He snapped his fingers. A thick **straw mattress** appeared on the iron bedstead. How it had come there Kasperl couldn't say. Zackleman snapped his fingers a second time, a third time and a fourth time. Now the bed had a **sheet**, a **pillow** and a **quilt** too.

"There, that will do", said the great magician. "I'm going to bed now. Good night, Seppel!"

"Good night, Great Magician Eprolisius Dagglepan."

Zackleman went away. His bedroom was in the **turret** of the castle, five floors up. However, Kasperl's room, like the kitchen, was on the ground floor. When he looked out of the window he could see the kitchen garden. Behind the kitchen garden lay the wood.

And the window ...?

The window was not **barred,** and it opened from inside.

"Not so bad!", thought Kasperl. "It looks as though the great magician will be peeling his own potatoes again tomorrow."

Kasperl waited until it was quite dark outside.

He wanted to set his friend Seppel free as soon as possible, after his escape. He would soon think how. The first thing was to get away from the castle.

Was Petrosilius Zackleman asleep yet?

Kasperl crept **cautiously** out of the window into the kitchen garden. He looked up at the castle. There were no lights; nothing was **stirring**. Good!

The garden fence was not particularly high. Yet when Kasperl tried to climb it a surprising thing happened. Someone **seized** his coat and his collar from behind and flung him back. Kasperl landed on all fours, rather hard.

Who had grabbed him? Was it the wicked magician Petrosilius Zackleman in person? Kasperl looked anxiously around, but there was no one at all in the kitchen garden.

"It must have been a trick", thought Kasperl. "I'll have another shot. I'll try a different place this time."

No sooner said than done.

Kasperl picked himself up and walked a few paces backwards. Then he took a run at the garden fence. He meant to swing himself over – but he failed again! This time someone collared him and hurled him back so hard that he plumped down on the ground like a sack of flour.

For a few minutes Kasperl lay where he had fallen – in the middle of Petrosilius Zackleman's **parsley bed**. He strained his ears, but there was nothing moving.

"Psst!", said Kasperl. "Is there anybody there?"

No answer.

"If there's anybody there, speak up!"

Everything was perfectly quiet. There was no sound but the rustle of leaves on the other side of the fence.

"I must have imagined it", thought Kasperl. "I'll have a third try ... I don't feel much like climbing over the fence now. I'll creep under it."

Kasperl crawled along the fence on hands and knees, looking for a gap. There was a loose **board** here! He could push it aside. The gap was big enough to let him through.

"Good!", thought Kasperl. He was going to crawl under the fence. But his luck was still out. Someone grabbed his feet and roughly **dragged him away**. There was more to come.

Suddenly there was a loud bang, and Kasperl had his ears boxed so hard that he cried out **in dismay**.

His yell awakened the great magician Petrosilius Zackleman. Petrosilius Zackleman put the light on and peered out of his bedroom window on the fifth floor. He was wearing a nightcap.

"Oho", he cried, "what's this I hear? What's this I see? Seppel's trying to escape! Well, well, what a silly thing to do, Seppel! You'll never be able to escape from my enchanted castle.

If you want to leave, either you need my permission – and I'll never give it to you – or you'll get exactly what you got just now. Go to bed, Seppel, and kindly don't disturb my beauty sleep any more – or else …"

A flash of lightning sizzled down and darted into the ground, inches away from Kasperl's toes. Kasperl was horribly frightened. In the castle turret, five floors up, the great magician Petrosilius Zackleman slammed the window shut with a **mocking** laugh.

What would you expect from a wicked magician like that?

to devour: verschlingen – helping: Portion – bedstead: Bettgestell – washstand: Waschtisch – straw mattress: Strohsack – sheet: Bettlaken – pillow: Kopfkissen – quilt: Steppdecke, Federbett – turret: Turm – barred: vergittert – cautious: vorsichtig – to stir: sich bewegen, rühren – to seize: ergreifen – no sooner said than done: gesagt, getan – parsley bed: Petersilienbeet – board: Latte, Brett – to drag s.b. away: jmd. wegzerren – in dismay: bestürzt, vor Schreck – mocking: spöttisch, höhnisch

As Stupid as Possible

Next morning Kasperl had to cook the magician a great **cauldron** full of potatoes. Zackleman never once laid down his spoon until the cauldron was empty. Then he wiped his mouth **contentedly** with the corner of his magic robe.

"What about me?", asked Kasperl, disappointed. He had hoped that Zackleman would leave him a few potatoes.

"Don't worry, my good fellow!"

The magician snapped his fingers. A loaf of bread, some butter and a **hunk** of cheese appeared by magic.

"That's for you, Seppel", he said. "But don't start eating yet. I've got something to say to you."

He cleared his throat.

"I shall have to **leave you on your own** today", he began. "I'm going to see another magician in Buxtehude. I shan't be back till late in the evening. If you feel hungry, go to the larder, and take what you want. The rest of the time you're to work. Now listen carefully. This is what you have to do. First, peel six saucepans full of potatoes and cut them into small pieces for supper. Second, **saw up** three loads of wood, split the logs and **stack** them. Third, scrub the kitchen floor. Fourth, dig the empty beds of earth in the kitchen garden. Repeat that!"

"Just as you say, Great Magician Spectrobilius Zigglespawn!", said Kasperl. He had decided to behave as stupidly as possible in future. He wanted to **infuriate** Zackleman. Perhaps the magician would get angry enough to kick Kasperl out of the castle.

So now Kasperl looked as if he were **racking his brains**. He rolled his eyes and scratched his head. Petrosilius Zackleman watched him for some time. Then he lost patience.

"Come along, come along!", he cried. "Can't you see I'm in a hurry? Open your mouth and tell me what you're supposed to do."

"What I'm to do?", said Kasperl. "I must ... Dear me, whatever was it now? I had it **on the tip of my tongue** a moment ago. But now ... wait a minute, I think I've got it."

Kasperl pushed Seppel's hat back on his head.

"First, saw up six saucepans full of potatoes, split them and stack them. Second, scrub three loads of wood. Third, peel the kitchen floor and cut it into small pieces for supper. Fourth ..."

"Shut up!", cried the great magician Petrosilius Zackleman. "Stop **talking rubbish**! Stop it at once!"

56

Kasperl looked very surprised.

"Stop?", he asked. "Why?"

"You're muddling everything up. You've got it all wrong. Now, begin again at the beginning!"

"Certainly, Great Magician Reprozilius Ficklespun! First, dig six saucepans full of potatoes. Second, saw up the kitchen floor, split it and stack it. Third, scrub the empty beds of earth in the kitchen garden. Fourth ... Now, what *was* fourth?"

"Nonsense!", shouted Petrosilius Zackleman. "**Utter nonsense!**"

"Why?", asked Kasperl.

"Why? Because you're stupid, that's why." Petrosilius Zackleman tapped his forehead. "**Solid bone** all through, that's your trouble. You can't even remember the simplest instructions. You're **driving** me **mad! Stark raving mad!**"

The great magician stamped his foot in a rage.

"This is it!", thought Kasperl. "Now he'll throw me out!"

But no.

The great magician Zackleman did not throw him out. He needed him. He snapped his fingers, and a bottle full of a dark liquid appeared by magic.

A drink from the bottle calmed him down.

"You're a **blockhead**, Seppel!", he said. "Well, it may be maddening in some ways, but there's no denying it has its advantages. Now – if you peel six saucepans full of potatoes by this evening, that will do. Peel them and cut them into small pieces, understand? I want fried potatoes for supper. You needn't do the rest of the work, you're too stupid. There

– and now I must hurry, or my friend in Buxtehude will think I've forgotten him. "

The great magician Petrosilius Zackleman hurried up to the platform on top of the castle turret. He spread his flowing magic robe on the floor. It was **embroidered** with red and yellow magic symbols. He sat down in the middle of the robe and recited a spell. The robe flew up in the air with him and carried him to Buxtehude.

As for Kasperl, when he had finished his bread and cheese, he set to work. He sat in the castle kitchen, peeling potatoes and thinking things over.

Most of all he thought about Seppel. Before they left the cave yesterday, the robber Hotzenplotz had **chained** Seppel to the wall by his left foot. He was left in the darkest corner of the cave, lying between the **barrel** of gunpowder and the barrel of pepper.

Was he still there, chained up, lying on the cold stone floor?

"Old Hotzenplotz might at least have given him a **blanket** or a bit of straw!", thought Kasperl.

The more Kasperl thought about it, the more he longed to know what had been happening to Seppel in the robber's cave ...

cauldron: Kessel – **contented**: zufrieden – **hunk**: Stück – **to leave s.b. on his own**: jmd. allein lassen – **larder**: Speisekammer – **to saw up**: zersägen – **to stack**: aufstapeln – **to infuriate**: wütend machen – **to rack one's brains**: sich den Kopf zerbrechen – **to have s.th. on the tip of one's tongue**: auf der Zunge liegen – **to talk rubbish**: Unsinn erzählen – **utter nonsense!**: Völliger Blödsinn! – **solid bone**: harter Knochen, strohdumm – **to drive mad**: verrückt machen – **stark raving mad**: total verrückt – **blockhead**: Dummkopf – **embroidered**: bestickt – **to chain**: anketten – **barrel**: Fass – **blanket**: Decke

For hours on end Seppel lay all alone in the robber's dark cave. Only the chain around his foot kept him from running away. But the chain would not come out of the wall. He shook it and tugged it with all his **might and main,** but it was no good. The chain was firmly fixed.

Toward evening Hotzenplotz came striding home again. He tipped the sack of snuff off his shoulder, flung his hat and coat into a corner and lit a candle.

"Well, Kasperl", he said, "you've been **lounging** here all day. Now you're going to work."

First Seppel had to take off the robber Hotzenplotz's dirty boots. Then Hotzenplotz unchained him.

"Go and light a fire on the **hearth.** I got myself a fat goose on the way home. When the fire's going, **pluck** the goose and pop it on the **spit**. I like it nice and crisp all over, and take care not to burn it! Meanwhile I'll make myself comfortable and put on my dressing gown."

Seppel plucked the goose and roasted it. The smell of the roasting **fowl** rose to his **nostrils** as he turned the spit. He had eaten nothing since breakfast; he felt quite weak with hunger. Would the robber Hotzenplotz leave a **morsel** for him?

The robber Hotzenplotz, however, intended to do no such thing! When the goose was done, he cried "Supper time!". Then he **gobbled up** the delicious goose, while Seppel went hungry. There wasn't so much as a bone left for Seppel to **gnaw**.

"Mm – that tasted good!", said the robber Hotzenplotz with a **belch** when he had finished. "Now I could do with a cup of coffee ..."

He went to his cupboard and took out a coffee mill. It was Grandmother's coffee mill! He filled it with coffee beans.

"There!", he said to Seppel. "Grind the coffee."

So Seppel had to grind coffee for Hotzenplotz in Grandmother's coffee mill. When he turned the handle the coffee mill played "Nuts in May".

That hurt – it hurt worse than anything else that had happened this unlucky day.

"What's the matter with you?", asked the robber Hotzenplotz, seeing tears spring to poor Seppel's eyes. "You look so sad, Kasperl. That won't do! Wait a minute – I'll cheer you up!"

He tore the pointed cap from Seppel's head.

"I don't like you in that silly cap. It doesn't **suit** you. There it goes!" He flung the cap into the fire and let it burn.

"Isn't that funny?", he cried. "It makes *me* laugh myself sick!"

Hotzenplotz roared with laughter. Seppel cried. He was still crying as he finished grinding the coffee, while Grandmother's coffee mill played "Nuts in May".

After that, Seppel had to clean and polish the robber's boots. Then he was chained up again. Hotzenplotz lay down and blew out the candle.

Half the night Seppel couldn't close his eyes. He felt so sad and homesick. He lay on the cold stone floor in between the barrel of gunpowder and the barrel of pepper, thinking about Kasperl. What would Kasperl say when he heard that the robber Hotzenplotz had burned his pointed cap? Or would Kasperl ever hear about it at all?

"Oh dear me", sighed Seppel. "What a dreadful mess we're in, me and poor Kasperl."

In the end he fell asleep. He dreamed of Kasperl and Grandmother. They were sitting in Grandmother's house having coffee and pie – plum pie, of course – with whipped cream. Kasperl was wearing his pointed cap, and everything was all right and everyone was happy. There was no chain around Seppel's foot, no robber's cave, and no Hotzenplotz.

If only his dream need never come to an end!

But it did come to an end, far too soon for poor Seppel. At six o'clock sharp in the morning the robber Hotzenplotz woke up. He roused Seppel.

"Hey, **lazybones!**", he cried. "Get up! It's time to start work."

There was coffee to grind, wood to chop, a fire to be lit. Then Hotzenplotz devoured his breakfast while Seppel had to stand by and watch. Breakfast had to be cleared away; then there was water to fetch, and **dishes to wash.** After that, Seppel had to turn the **grindstone** while Hotzenplotz sharpened his curved sword and his seven knives.

"Get a move on, **slowcoach!**", shouted the robber. "This is a grindstone, not a **barrel organ!** Faster, faster!"

When all the knives were sharpened, Seppel had to creep

back to his corner and be chained up. Then the robber Hotzenplotz threw him a **stale crust** of bread.

"There – eat that, Kasperl, just so you don't starve to death. I'm going to work now, the same as every day. You can take it easy and get some rest. You'll have to work all the harder for me when I come home this evening! Why should you have a better time than your friend Seppel is having with the wicked magician Petrosilius Zackleman?"

With that he left the robber's cave and shut the door behind him.

The mean old ruffian!

for hours on end: stundenlang – **with might and main:** mit aller Kraft – **to lounge:** faulenzen – **hearth:** Herd – **to pluck:** rupfen – **spit:** Spieß – **fowl:** Geflügel – **nostril:** Nasenloch – **morsel:** Happen – **to gobble up:** verschlingen – **to gnaw:** abnagen – **belch:** Rülpser – **to suit:** passen, stehen – **lazybones:** Faulpelz – **to wash the dishes:** abspülen – **grindstone:** Schleifstein – **slowcoach:** Transuse – **barrel organ:** Drehorgel – **stale:** vertrocknet, alt – **crust:** Kanten – **ruffian:** Schuft

Three Doors in the Cellar

When Kasperl had peeled three saucepans full of potatoes he stopped for a rest. He put down his knife, wiped his wet hands on his trousers, and then he went to see what he could find to eat in the magician's larder. It must be nearly dinner time, and he was feeling hungry.

The first thing that met his eyes was a jar of **pickled gherkins**.

"People say sour food makes you merry!", he thought. "This should be the right stuff for me then!"

Kasperl ate three gherkins. After that he felt much better.

He tasted all the different pots of jam that stood side by side in the cupboard. Then he drank a glass of buttermilk, and finally he cut himself a slice of salami sausage. Zackleman had sausages and ham in his larder, too – all kinds of sausages were hanging from the ceiling, long ones and short ones, thin ones and fat ones. All Kasperl had to do was reach out his hand.

"It's like fairyland!", thought Kasperl.

But as he stood there **gaping** at the sausages he suddenly heard a deep **sobbing** sound.

"Boo-hooo!"

Kasperl was terror-stricken. Wasn't he alone in the enchanted castle after all? Was there someone else here too – and if so, who?

"Oh well!", thought Kasperl. "Never mind!"

He **carved** a piece of sausage and put it in his mouth. Then he heard the sobbing again.

"Boo-hooo!"

It was a low, sad sobbing – so sad that the mere sound of it took away Kasperl's appetite. There really was someone there. Someone who seemed to be in terrible trouble.

"I wonder if I could help?", thought Kasperl. "I'll have to find out what's wrong! I can't just stand here listening. It makes me feel quite depressed!"

Kasperl **strained his ears** to find where the sobbing came from. He followed the sound from the larder back into the kitchen, from the kitchen out into the hall, and so to the cellar door.

"Boo-hoo-hooo!", Kasperl heard.

The noise came from the cellar. Should he **pluck up his courage** and go down?

"Coming!", he called. "I must just get a light."

He ran back to the kitchen and took the **lantern** down from its hook over the **sink**. He struck a match and put it to the **wick**, and then he was ready.

He clambered carefully down the slippery steps. The cellar was **damp** and **musty**. Kasperl shivered. Big drops of moisture fell from the ceiling, splashing on his hat. He found himself in a long, low passage, and after ten **paces** or so he came to a door.

The door was **studded** with iron. There was a notice with a black border, saying:

NO ENTRY

Kasperl hesitated for a moment. Then he heard the sobbing again, and knew that he had to go on. He turned the handle and opened the door.

But what now? Directly behind the first door he found a second door. This one was studded with iron, too. And there was another big notice with a black border. Kasperl raised his lantern and read:

"Help!", thought Kasperl. "There's less and less entry the farther I go."

However, he plucked up his courage once more. He heard the **mournful** sobs again, and he opened the second door.

But still he had not reached the last door! A few more paces, and he came to a third door. This door, too, had a big notice with a black border, saying:

Kasperl had a **quivering, sinking feeling** in his stomach. Was it fright – or was it just the gherkins and buttermilk?

"Wouldn't it be better to turn back?", he said to himself.

Then he heard the sobbing again, behind the third door. This time it sounded so **dreary** and miserable that it went to Kasperl's heart. He forgot all about his fright and the pain in his stomach.

He stepped forward, grasped the door knob – and the third door swung open, creaking and groaning horribly.

and the third door swung open, creaking and groaning

pickled gherkins: saure Gurken – **to gape:** hinaufstarren, emporschauen – **to sob:** schluchzen – **to carve:** absäbeln – **to strain one's ears:** die Ohren spitzen, lauschen – **to pluck up one's courage:** sich ein Herz fassen – **lantern:** Laterne – **sink:** Spülbecken – **wick:** Docht – **damp:** feucht – **musty:** modrig – **pace:** Schritt – **to stud:** beschlagen – **mournful:** kläglich – **quivering, sinking feeling:** flaues Gefühl – **dreary:** trüb, schaurig

The Mysterious Toad

"Stop! Stay where you are! Don't come any closer!"

Kasperl had hardly crossed the **threshold** when a harsh voice **croaked** these words. He was sure it was the same voice that had been sobbing.

Kasperl **obeyed**, and stopped just where he was.

In the light of the lantern he saw that he was in a small, dark cellar. But the cellar had no floor. Right before Kasperl's feet the ground fell away to a deep pool of dark water.

Kasperl instinctively shrank back and leaned against the doorpost.

"Is there anyone there?", he asked. He hardly recognized his own voice, it sounded so deep and hollow.

There was a splashing, gurgling noise down in the pool.

"Yes, there is someone here," croaked the voice. "If you lie flat on the ground and look down you can see me."

Kasperl obeyed the voice again.

Lying flat on the ground he inched his way to the side of the pool, and looked over the edge, holding the lantern in his outstretched hand.

"I can't see you. Where are you?"

"Down here in the water. You must hold the lantern a little lower."

There was something swimming in the dark water. It had huge **goggle-eyes** and a big, wide mouth.

"Well?", it croaked. "You can see me now, can't you?"

"Yes, I can see you now", said Kasperl.

"And what would you call me?"

"If you were a bit smaller, I'd say you were a **frog**."

"Wrong. I'm a toad."

"Oh", said Kasperl, thinking the creature looked rather big for a toad, too. "What are you doing down there?", he added out loud.

"Waiting."

"What for?"

"I'm waiting for someone to set me free. You must know that I'm not really a toad. I'm – I'm –"

"Well, what?", asked Kasperl.

"I don't know if I can trust you", croaked the toad who said it was not a toad. "Did Zackleman send you?"

"No", said Kasperl. "Zackleman doesn't know I'm here. He's gone to see another magician in Buxtehude."

The toad heaved a great sigh. "Are you sure?", it asked.

"Positive", said Kasperl. "**Cross my heart.** Now, if you're not a toad, tell me what you are!"

"Once upon a time I was a good **fairy**", said the toad.

"A fairy?"

"Yes, the fairy Amaryllis. But seven years ago I was turned into a toad and I've been sitting in this **pond** ever since. Boo-hooo! Zackleman cast a spell over me and shut me up here."

"Seven years!", cried Kasperl. "How **dreadful**! Why did Zackleman do it?"

"Because he's so wicked. He hates me, just because I sometimes **interfered with** his magic a little. I was too kind to him – that was how he got the better of me and turned me into a toad. A – boo-hooo! – a toad!"

The enchanted fairy wept bitterly. Big tears ran down her toad face. Kasperl wanted to comfort her; he felt so sorry for her. But what could he do?

"Can I help you?", he asked.

"Oh yes, yes, you can!", sobbed the toad, wiping away the tears with her foot. "All you have to do is find a certain herb called **fairyweed**. It grows on the open **heath** a few miles from this castle. If you bring some of this herb and touch me with it I shall be free. It dissolves wicked spells at once. Will you get it for me? Why don't you answer me?"

"Because ...", said Kasperl. He stopped.

"Well? Because what?"

"Because I can't get out of here. I'm shut up in this en- chanted castle, too. I'll tell you all about it."

Kasperl told the toad about his adventures the night before. He told her how he had tried to escape three times. "If you can tell me how to get out", he finished, "I'll bring you the fairyweed. But I'm afraid you won't know how."

"What makes you think so?", croaked the frog. "I was once a fairy, remember. I know a few things about magic. You can't escape from the castle because Zackleman has drawn a magic circle around it. But if you leave any of your clothes behind in the castle – something you wear next to your skin – you'll be free to go wherever you like."

"Really and truly?", asked Kasperl.

"Try and see", croaked the toad. "You'll soon find that I've told you the truth. Your shirt would be the best thing to leave, but your hat will do, or one of your **stockings**."

"My hat?", asked Kasperl. "It's only **borrowed**. It belongs to my friend, not me."

"That doesn't matter. It comes to the same thing."

"Then of course I shall leave the hat behind", said Kasperl. "I shan't miss it because it doesn't fit me anyway. Now, tell me what this fairyweed looks like and where to find it. Then I will fetch it for you."

toad: Unke – **threshold**: Schwelle – **to croak**: quaken – **to obey**: gehorchen – **goggle-eyes**: Glotzaugen – **frog**: Frosch – **cross my heart**: Ehrenwort – **fairy**: Fee – **pond**: Teich, Pfuhl – **dreadful**: entsetzlich – **to interfere with**: stören – **fairyweed**: Feenkraut – **heath**: Heide – **stocking**: Strumpf – **to borrow**: borgen, leihen

The Open Heath

Kasperl made the fairy tell him exactly how to reach the open heath.

"When you get there", said the toad, "sit down under the old **pine tree** that stands alone by the dark pond on the heath. Wait there until the moon rises. You can only find fairyweed by moonlight. In the light of the moon it begins to shine; then you can see the little silver flowers gleaming among the roots of the pine. When you have picked a **bunch** of them you will be safe. Even Zackleman can do you no harm then – anyone who holds fairyweed in his hand is invisible to the wicked magician."

"Do you think he'll look for me when he comes home and finds me gone?"

"I'm sure he will. So you must try to pick a bunch of fairy-weed as soon as possible. Off with you now. There's a long way to go. Good luck – very, *very* good luck!"

Kasperl stood up and waved his lantern to the toad down in the pool.

"Goodbye!", he said.

"Goodbye! Don't forget to shut the doors behind you. Zackleman must not know that you've been talking to me."

To be sure, the doors! Kasperl had quite forgotten them. He closed them all behind him and climbed the cellar steps. He closed the cellar door too. Then he took a piece of bread and two sausages from the magician's larder and started out.

He climbed through the window of his room into the kitchen garden. Then he took off his hat. He was not at all sorry to part with it, and put it down in the parsley bed, quite near the fence.

Would it work this time? He didn't feel particularly happy, thinking of last night and the way his ears had been boxed.

"Oh well, I'll try it", he said to himself. "I can't do worse than before."

But this time everything went smoothly. No unseen hand took Kasperl by the collar and hauled him back; no one boxed his ears. Breathing a sigh of relief, he dropped on to the grass on the far side of the fence.

"Ooff!", said Kasperl. "I'd never have thought that hat of Seppel's would come in so useful!"

And now for the open heath.

Kasperl walked for several hours. He kept following the

way the toad had described; first through the wood, then a little way along the high road, then on beside a **brook** until he reached another wood. There should be three **birch trees** here, and the middle tree should have a split **trunk**.

Yes, there they were! And there was a footpath leading into the wood, just as the toad had said. Now Kasperl had to follow this path. It was two hours more before he came to the open heath, and by this time evening was gradually drawing in.

Kasperl was glad he had found the place at last. He sat down under the pine tree beside the dark pond, took off his shoes and stockings, dangled his tired legs in the water and waited for the moon to rise. To pass the time he ate the bread and both the sausages.

He tried hard not to think of the great magician Petrosilius Zackleman, but he couldn't help it. The longer he sat and waited, the more uncomfortable he felt.

Was Zackleman back from Buxtehude yet? What would he do when he found that Kasperl had disappeared?

"Oh, where *are* you, moon?", sighed Kasperl. "Aren't you ever going to rise? If Zackleman finds me before I've picked the fairyweed, it's all up. Can you hear me, moon? Come on, do come on!"

But the moon was taking her time. She simply would not rise. Kasperl **was on tenterhooks**, thinking of Petrosilius Zackleman.

---

pine tree: Fichte – **bunch**: Bund, Büschel – **brook**: Bach – **birch tree**: Birke – **trunk**: Stamm – **to be on tenterhooks**: wie auf Nadeln/glühenden Kohlen sitzen

"The Owner of the Hat"

Between eight o'clock and half past eight in the evening the wicked magician Petrosilius Zackleman flew home from Buxtehude on his magic robe. He was as hungry as a hunter. It had been a tiring day, but now that he was home he could **eat to his heart's content**. He hoped the fried potatoes were ready – and he hoped there were plenty of them.

The great magician landed on the castle turret. He went straight down to the dining-room, sat down at the table, tucked a **napkin** under his chin and clapped his hands.

"Seppel!", he shouted. "Serve the fried potatoes!"

There was a long silence. Nothing moved.

"Seppel!", cried Zackleman. "Serve the fried potatoes! Can't you hear me? Where are you?"

80

Still nothing happened.

"Just you wait, lazybones!", raged the great magician. "Shall I **stir you up** a bit? This is too much!"

He snapped his fingers and wished for a **whip**. Then he ran to the kitchen.

"Come here, you **scoundrel**!", he thundered. "I'll beat you black and blue! How dare you, you **wretched imp**? Keep the great magician Zackleman waiting, would you? Come here, you **idler**! I'll beat you to a jelly! I'll **wallop** you till you can't sit down."

In his fury the great magician **thwacked** the kitchen table several times with his whip. Only then did he notice that there were still three saucepans full of unpeeled potatoes standing on the table.

"What!", he cried. "What's all this? Run away from work, have you? Thunder and lightning, I'll see you don't play any more tricks like this. Come here! Come here this minute!"

But though he raged and shouted and hit the table it did him no good at all.

"Aha!", gnarled the great magician. "Now I know where the fellow must be hiding! But I shall find him. Oh yes – I shall find him all right, and then he'll learn to know me better!"

Petrosilius Zackleman snapped his fingers. The whip changed into a lighted **torch**. Holding the torch above his head Zackleman went right through the castle. He looked in all the living-rooms and all the bedrooms. He went to the cellars and up to the attics. He shone his torch into every corner, he searched **every nook and cranny**, he looked under the furniture and behind the curtains. But though he searched and searched he found no trace of Kasperl at all.

Suddenly the great magician had an idea. He hurried out into the kitchen garden as fast as his legs would carry him. Sure enough, there lay Seppel's hat in the middle of the parsley bed, not far from the fence.

"Fire and pestilence!"

The great magician Zackleman **clenched his fists** and **spat** on the earth. The moment he set eyes on the hat he realized what had happened. That wretched Seppel had managed to escape, stupid as he was!

How did he know the secret?

"However he knew, I must act quickly!", thought Petrosilius Zackleman. "He'll be surprised to find how soon I have him in my power again, now that I've found his hat!"

In fact, it was easy for Petrosilius Zackleman to bring anyone to his castle by magic so long as he had something the person wore.

"To work!", cried the great magician grimly, throwing his torch aside.

He seized Seppel's hat with both hands and ran to his study. Where was his magic **chalk**? Quick – he drew a magic circle. Then he drew lines across it.

"There – now we can begin!"

Petrosilius Zackleman put the hat in the middle of the magic circle, just where all the lines met. Then he stepped back, raised his hands and waved them about in the air. Keeping his eyes on the hat, he **chanted** in a loud voice:

"Come to me, come to me.
Come, wherever you may be!
Let the owner of the hat be here.
Where the hat is let the man appear.
Abracadabra!"

The great magician Petrosilius Zackleman had hardly finished reciting this spell when there was a mighty crash. A bright flame shot up from the study floor. And in the middle of the magic circle, just where all the lines crossed, stood – Seppel.

The real Seppel.

The one who owned the hat.

Seppel was holding a black leather boot in his left hand and a shoe brush in his right hand.

Exactly as the spell said – "the owner of the hat" had appeared.

It would be hard to say who looked sillier at that moment, Kasperl's friend Seppel or the wicked magician Petrosilius Zackleman.

to eat to one's heart's content: sich satt essen – napkin: Serviette – to stir s.b. up: jmd. Beine machen – whip: Peitsche – scoundrel: Schurke, Satansbraten – wretched imp: erbärmlicher Wicht – idler: Faulpelz – to wallop: verhauen – to thwack: auf etwas schlagen – torch: Fackel – every nook and cranny: jeder Winkel – to clench one's fists: die Fäuste ballen – to spit: spucken – chalk: Kreide – to chant: singen

A Magician of his Word

Only a moment ago Seppel had been cleaning the robber Hotzenplotz's boots – and now here he was, all of a sudden, face to face with the great magician Petrosilius Zackleman. How on earth did he come to be in this castle instead of the robber's cave? And how did he get there? Seppel felt as **dazed** as if he had tumbled down from the moon.

Petrosilius Zackleman himself looked rather **taken aback**. What was this perfect stranger doing in his magic circle? Something must have gone wrong. Such a thing had never happened in all the time he had been working magic. And he had been working magic for fifty years, at least.

"Who are you, for goodness' sake?", **gasped** the great magician.

"Me?", asked Seppel.

"Yes, you!", **spat** Zackleman. "And how did you get here?"

"I've no idea how I got here. But I'm Seppel."

"You're Seppel? Seppel, did you say? You can't be."

"Why not?"

"Why not?", growled Petrosilius Zackleman. "Because you don't look a bit like Seppel. Let me tell you, I *know* Seppel. He was my servant. That hat over there – ", he pointed to Seppel's hat lying on the floor in the middle of the magic circle, "that's *his* hat."

"That hat?", asked Seppel. Suddenly light dawned on him. He had to laugh.

"You'd laugh, would you?", cried the great magician. "What's the joke?"

"Well, now I know who you mean. You mean Kasperl! Just like the robber Hotzenplotz! He got me and Kasperl mixed up, too."

Petrosilius Zackleman pricked up his ears. He made Seppel tell him how he and Kasperl had changed hats. Gradually he realized how it had all happened. So Hotzenplotz had sold him Kasperl, thinking that Kasperl was Seppel! A fine story! No wonder his magic spell with Seppel's hat could produce only the real Seppel, not the wrong one.

"Sulphur and brimstone!"

The great magician was **foaming** at the mouth. What a mess the robber Hotzenplotz had got him into! But there was still a way out. All he needed was Kasperl's pointed cap. Then he could bring Kasperl there by magic too.

He had to take care not to make Seppel suspicious. Petrosilius Zackleman thought of a clever trick.

"Do you think I'm going to believe that you're really Seppel?", he said. "Prove it!"

"Certainly", said Seppel, "just tell me how."

"Well – I'll believe you if you give me Kasperl's cap."

"Kasperl's cap?", said Seppel. "Oh, I can't do that."

"Why not?"

"Well, you see, the robber Hotzenplotz has burned it."

"Burned it?", cried Zackleman.

"That's right", said Seppel. "He threw it in the fire before my very eyes. From **sheer spite.**"

"Spite?" The great magician's fist crashed down on the table. "Stupidity! Idiocy! Oh, Hotzenplotz, you stupid **imbecile!** You'll drive me mad!" Petrosilius Zackleman ran up and down his study several times, shouting with rage.

Then he stopped in front of Seppel. "Whose boot are you holding?", he asked. "Does it belong to Hotzenplotz?"

"Yes", said Seppel.

"Then give it to me! I'll soon get hold of the **wretch!**"

Hurriedly Petrosilius Zackleman drew another magic circle. This time he put the robber Hotzenplotz's boot on the place where the lines crossed. He raised his arms and waved them in the air again, calling in a voice of thunder:

"Come to me, come to me.
Come wherever you may be.
Let the owner of the boot be here
Where the boot is let the man appear.
Abracadabra!"

For the second time the magic spell worked. There was a crash, a flame shot up – and there stood the robber Hotzenplotz in the middle of the magic circle, looking as if he had grown out of the floor. He was wearing his warm **dressing gown,** and he had no shoes on. At first he looked absurdly **puzzled.** Then he began to laugh.

"Zackleman!", he cried. "Ha, ha, old friend – what a joker you are! That's magic for you! He just casts a spell and **spirits** me from my cave to his study! – Why, look, Kasperl's here too! I was just racking my brains to think where he could have gone ..."

"Shut up!", interrupted the great magician Petrosilius Zackleman. "In the first place, this is Seppel, not Kasperl. In the second place, stop laughing in that silly way this minute, or I might forget myself."

"Whatever's wrong with you, Zackleman, old fellow?", asked the robber Hotzenplotz. "Why are you **in** such **a temper?**"

"I'll tell you what's wrong! The lad you sold me yesterday has escaped. He wasn't the stupid Seppel at all. He was Kasperl."

"Well, imagine that!", said Hotzenplotz. "But you're a great magician. Why don't you bring the runaway back by magic?"

"Exactly what I *would* have done by this time, if I could. But I can't."

"Can't you?", inquired Hotzenplotz.

"No, I can't", said Petrosilius Zackleman. "And why not?

Because you went and burned his cap! It's enough to drive me crazy. Oh, you **cuckoo** of a robber, you silly cuckoo!"

Hotzenplotz drew himself up.

"Zackleman!", he cried. "I won't put up with that sort of language. You're going too far. Me – a cuckoo? You will kindly take that back!"

"You think so?" The great magician bared his teeth in a grin and snapped his fingers for his magic staff. "If I called you a silly cuckoo I was quite right. I'm a magician of my word. Abracadabra ..."

He **muttered** a spell, and Hotzenplotz turned into a cuckoo. A real cuckoo, making frightened noises and hopping from one leg to another, flapping its wings.

"Never thought of that one, did you?", **mocked** Zackleman. "Wait a minute, there's more to come!"

He snapped his fingers, and a **birdcage** appeared by magic. He seized the cuckoo and put it inside the cage.

"There, my friend, you can sit there and wonder what's to become of you. And now for you, Seppel!"

Seppel had been watching in fear and trembling while the robber Hotzenplotz was changed into a cuckoo. Now the great magician turned to him. His heart fell into his boots. He felt sure that Petrosilius Zackleman was going to cast a spell on him.

However, he was wrong.

"Can you peel potatoes?", asked the great magician.

"Yes", said Seppel, who couldn't see where this question was leading.

"Good. Off you go to the castle kitchen then. When I come home tomorrow morning I want to have fried potatoes. You can hang the birdcage up in the kitchen. Make Hotzenplotz sing to you while you work. When you've peeled twelve saucepans full of potatoes and cut them into small pieces, you can lie down and go to sleep, but not before."

"What about you?", asked Seppel.

"I'm going to fly on my magic robe and look for Kasperl. He'll never slip through my fingers! I shall find him, as sure as I'm the great magician Petrosilius Zackleman – and then I shall make mincemeat of him!"

dazed: verdattert – taken aback: erstaunt, belämmert – to gasp: schnauben – to spit: fauchen – sulphur and brimstone!: Pech und Schwefel! – to foam: schäumen, Gift und Galle spucken – sheer spite: pure Bosheit – imbecile: Dummkopf – wretch: Unglückswurm, armer Wicht – dressing gown: Morgenmantel – puzzled: verdutzt – to spirit: (an einen Ort) zaubern – to be in a temper: schlecht gelaunt, grantig sein – cuckoo: Kuckuck, Einfaltspinsel – to mutter: murmeln – to mock: spotten – birdcage: Vogelkäfig

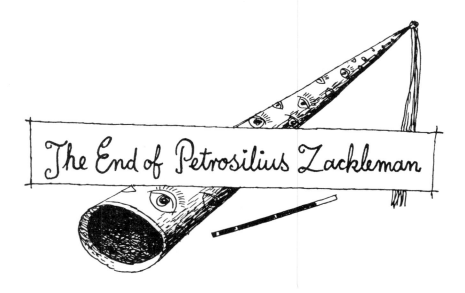

The End of Petrosilius Zackleman

The great magician Petrosilius Zackleman put on his night-time spectacles, so as to see better in the dark. Then he hurried up to the castle turret, mounted his magic robe and took off.

He flew all over the countryside, keeping a sharp lookout, but all **in vain**. He could find no trace of Kasperl.

While all this was going on, the moon had risen over the open heath. The fairyweed immediately began to gleam with a silvery light among the roots of the old pine tree. Quickly Kasperl picked a bunch of the flowers. Now Petrosilius Zackleman couldn't see him, even with his special night-time spectacles.

Kasperl set off to walk back, holding the fairyweed in his pocket with his right hand. Twice – three times – Zackleman flew by overhead on his magic robe. Kasperl **hunched** his shoulders and ducked his head. Even if he had not ducked, Zackleman couldn't have seen him, although the magician was flying so low that Kasperl felt the rush of air as he passed.

The fairyweed made him invisible, but that was not all. Now that the **herb** was in his pocket, Kasperl didn't feel tired any longer. His legs seemed to be walking **of their own accord**. In the faint light of dawn he reached the castle **safe and sound**.

The gate was shut. Kasperl touched it with the fairyweed and it opened to let him in. At that very moment he heard a tremendous rushing sound in the air above him. Looking up, he saw that Zackleman had just landed on the castle turret. He hoped that Zackleman had not noticed anything peculiar.

But the wicked magician Petrosilius Zackleman *had* noticed something. A few minutes ago the gate of his castle had opened and shut again all by itself.

"Oho!", he exclaimed. "**Goblins** and **hobgoblins**, what's all this? Someone I can't see has come into my castle. But who? And poisonous snakes, how did he do it?"

Petrosilius Zackleman snapped his fingers for his magic staff.

"Whoever it is", he cried in a fury, "I'll find him. I'll punish him for his **impertinence**. Thunder and lightning, sulphur and brimstone, I'll punish him horribly!"

The great magician ran down the **spiral staircase** to the ground floor, three steps at a time. By this time Kasperl was on his way to the cellar. He was running down the dark passage towards the toad's pool. He had no lantern this time, but he didn't need one; with the fairyweed in his hand he could see in the dark like a cat. The first door – then the second door – and now the third door ...

"Here I am!", he cried. "I've got it. Tell me what to do."

"Give me your hand and help me out."

Kasperl lay flat on the floor and stretched out the hand holding the fairyweed to the toad in the pool.

"No, the other one!", croaked the toad. "You must help me out of the water first."

Kasperl could hear a loud, angry voice just outside the cellar. Petrosilius Zackleman had noticed that the cellar door was open, and a terrible suspicion flashed into his mind. **Cursing** and raging, he clattered down the steps. It would be only a matter of minutes before he reached them.

"Quick!", cried the toad.

Kasperl seized her with his left hand and put her down on the floor beside him. Zackleman was coming nearer and nearer. The cellar echoed with his shouts and screams of fury.

"Quick!", said the toad again. "Touch me with the fairyweed."

Kasperl obeyed.

At that moment the wicked magician Petrosilius Zackleman stormed through the last door. But all of a sudden he **stopped dead** in his tracks.

And when great magicians stop dead in their tracks, their time is almost up . . .

Kasperl was frightened too – but not at the sight of the wicked magician. He was afraid of the light that flooded the cellar. It was a blinding light. Kasperl had to close his eyes. When he opened them again he saw a beautiful lady standing beside him.

She shone like the sun. Everything about her was so beautiful that Kasperl could hardly take it all in – her face, her hands, her hair and her long golden dress.

"Oh!", thought Kasperl. "I'll be dazzled if I look any longer ... "

Should he look away? But he couldn't look away either. So he **prudently** closed one eye and looked at the fairy out of the other.

Petrosilius Zackleman was standing by the cellar wall as if he had been **struck by lightning**. His face was white as chalk, his knees were knocking, big drops of moisture ran down his face. He tried to speak, but he had lost his voice. He was so dazed that the magic staff slapped from his hand.

The staff fell to the ground. The fairy Amaryllis touched it lightly with the **toe** of her shoe. It rolled over and over and fell into the pool with a splash.

At last Petrosilius Zackleman plucked up his courage.

"Curses on you!", he screamed.

He jumped forward to save the magic staff. Too late! His fingers grabbed the empty air. He lost his footing, overbalanced – and before Kasperl and the fairy Amaryllis could help him he plunged into the deep water.

There was a last terrible scream.

Then he was swallowed up. Gurgling and bubbling, the deep water of the toad's pool closed over the wicked magician Petrosilius Zackleman.

in vain: umsonst – **to hunch:** hochziehen – **herb:** Kraut – **of its own accord:** wie von selbst – **safe and sound:** wohlbehalten – **goblin, hobgoblin:** Kobold, Gespenst – **impertinence:** Unverschämtheit – **spiral staircase:** Wendeltreppe – **to curse:** fluchen – **to stop dead:** erstarren – **prudently:** vorsichtshalber – **to be struck by lightning:** vom Blitz getroffen, vom Donner gerührt – **toe:** (Fuß-)Spitze

A Fairy Lady

Seppel had been peeling potatoes half the night. It was very difficult to keep awake, but he was too frightened of the great magician Zackleman to go to sleep. Not until the last potato was peeled and cut up did he **slump forward** on the kitchen stool, when he fell asleep **on the spot**.

Seppel slept with his head resting on the edge of the table. In his dreams he was still at work. There was a great mountain of potatoes in front of him; he went on and on peeling them, but he never came to the end. The mountain never looked any smaller, in fact it was growing bigger and broader.

At last Petrosilius Zackleman came into the castle kitchen. When he saw that poor Seppel was still peeling potatoes he began to **scold** him. He raged and stormed so furiously that Seppel tumbled off the stool – and woke up.

He sat on the kitchen floor rubbing his eyes. He saw that the sun had risen, and realized that he had been dreaming. But Zackleman's fury had not been a dream – that was real enough! The whole enchanted castle was echoing with his roars of rage.

The cuckoo in the birdcage had awakened, too. It was fluttering about calling "Cuckoo! Cuckoo!" until Seppel was **deafened**.

"Shut your **beak!**", cried Seppel.

He went to the kitchen door to listen. What could be wrong? Why was the great magician making all that noise?

Suddenly Petrosilius Zackleman stopped shouting. For a while everything was absolutely quiet. Then the voice of the great magician rang out again. He sounded angrier than ever this time. But it lasted only for a moment or so.

"What can be the matter?", thought Seppel.

He turned the door knob, opened the door, and went out into the hall.

There was no one there, no sound to be heard ...

Wait a minute – a light was shining on the cellar steps. There were voices. Someone was climbing the steps. It was not the great magician Petrosilius Zackleman. It was Kasperl!

Seppel shouted for joy, and ran to meet Kasperl with open arms.

"Kasperl!"

He was so pleased he could have **squashed** Kasperl **flat**.

"Seppel!", cried Kasperl. "I thought you were in the robber's cave. What are you doing here?"

"Me?", said Seppel. "I've been peeling potatoes. And now I'm as happy as a king! But tell me ..."

Suddenly Seppel caught sight of the fairy Amaryllis. She had followed Kasperl up the cellar steps. Seppel's eyes and mouth fell wide open when he saw her.

"Who's that lady?", he asked.

"She's a fairy lady", said Kasperl. "The fairy Amaryllis."

"What a lovely name! It's just right for her."

"Do you think so?", said the fairy Amaryllis, smiling. "But who are *you*?"

"Him?", said Kasperl, for Seppel was too **amazed** to answer. "He's my friend Seppel. The best friend in the whole world. I don't know what he's doing here, though; he'll have to tell me himself. Go on, Seppel!"

However, the fairy Amaryllis interrupted. "He can tell you outside", she said. "Come out with me. Now that Petrosilius Zackleman is dead, his castle must not be left standing."

"What are you going to do?", asked Kasperl.

"Wait and see", said the fairy Amaryllis. She took Kasperl by one hand and Seppel by the other. She was going to lead the two friends out of the castle.

But Seppel let go of her hand.

"Wait a minute", he said. "I've got to fetch something."

He ran to the kitchen and took down the birdcage.

"What!", said Kasperl, when Seppel joined them again. "A bird?"

"That's right", said Seppel, grinning, "it's a cuckoo – rather a funny sort of cuckoo."

Then they both followed the fairy Amaryllis out of the castle gate. Once they were outside, the fairy told them to go a little farther away, as far as the wood. She herself stayed behind. When Kasperl and Seppel had reached the wood, she turned to the castle and raised her hand. The walls silently crumpled and fell. There was nothing left of Zackleman's enchanted castle but a **heap** of broken stones and **tiles**. The toad's pool was hurled beneath the ruins. The fairy Amaryllis made a **hedge** of thorns grow up around the ruins of the castle. Then she turned her back on the ruin and went up to the two friends. She didn't walk; she **floated**. The leaves and grass dipped down as she passed over them.

"I have to thank you, Kasperl", she said. "You can be sure I shall never forget what you have done for me."

She took a thin gold ring from her finger.

"Take this ring and keep it safe", she said. "It is a wishing ring. It will give you three wishes. Whatever they are, if you say them aloud and turn the ring on your finger, they will be **granted**. Now give me your hand, Kasperl."

Kasperl let the fairy Amaryllis put the ring on his finger. He said "Thank you". But the fairy Amaryllis said that she was the one who should be thanking him.

"Now I am going home to fairyland", she said. "Goodbye, both of you, good luck, and a safe return home! I wish you health and happiness and merry hearts, today, tomorrow and always!"

With these words she floated away. Kasperl and Seppel waved their handkerchiefs. As she flew she began to look thin and transparent, until at last she faded away altogether and vanished out of sight.

to slump forward: nach vorne kippen –
on the spot: auf der Stelle – **to scold:**
schimpfen – **to deafen:** taub machen –
beak: Schnabel – **to squash flat:** zu Mus
quetschen – **amazed:** erstaunt, verblüfft
– **heap:** Haufen – **tile:** Dachziegel –
hedge: Hecke – **to float:** schweben – **to
grant:** erfüllen

A Wishing Ring

It was some time before Kasperl and Seppel could speak a word. Then they both began talking at once. They both shouted at the tops of their voices for several minutes. Kasperl was shouting at Seppel and Seppel was shouting at Kasperl. Each of them was telling his own story and neither was listening to the other. Kasperl gave up first. He put his hand over Seppel's mouth.

"Hey, stop!", he cried. "This is no good. We must take turns."

"All right", said Seppel. "Let's count our **buttons** to see who is first. Right?"

They both began counting their coat buttons.

"Me – you – me – you ..."

As it happened they each had five buttons on their coats. "Me!", said Seppel when he got to the fifth button. At once he started telling his story all over again. But Kasperl, too, said "Me!" when he counted *his* fifth button, so there they were, both talking at once again.

"I tell you what", said Seppel, realizing that something must have gone wrong. "We'll have to do it another way. Let's try a counting-out rhyme – that ought to work!"

He solemnly licked his forefinger three times. Pointing to Kasperl and himself in turn he counted:

"Eeny – meeny – miny – mo ..."

He finished up pointing at Kasperl; so now it was settled.

"Well then", said Kasperl. "Just listen to this, Seppel ..."

Kasperl told Seppel all his adventures from beginning to end. He was **talking a mile a minute**. As Seppel listened, his ears went scarlet and he grew hot with excitement. He hung on Kasperl's words, hardly daring to breathe. When Kasperl told him about the dreadful end of Petrosilius Zackleman, he clapped his hands together.

"Oh, Kasperl!", he cried. "If only I'd known!"

"Why?", asked Kasperl.

"Well, if I'd known I'd never have spent half the night peeling potatoes for him."

Then it was Seppel's turn. He told Kasperl what a bad time he had had in the robber's cave – and how Hotzenplotz had burned Kasperl's cap.

"What? My beautiful cap?", cried Kasperl furiously. "This

is too much! We must put that **brute** Hotzenplotz **behind bars**."

Seppel decided that this was the right moment.

"Calm down", he said quietly. "He *is* behind bars!"

"Behind bars –?", asked Kasperl.

"He's in this cage. He's the cuckoo. You do look surprised, Kasperl! I'll tell you all about it."

Seppel went on with his story. When he finished, Kasperl was hot with excitement too.

"How lucky that it turned out all right in the end!", he cried. "And now what?"

"Now let's take the cuckoo to Sergeant Dimplemoser. Then we'll go home."

Seppel swung the birdcage happily back and forth. He was ready to start. But Kasperl did not move.

"First I need a new cap!", he explained.

"Where are you going to find one?"

"We've got a wishing ring, remember!"

Kasperl turned the ring on his finger.

"I wish for a new pointed cap, just like the old one", he said. The words were hardly out of his mouth before his wish was granted.

You see how useful it is
to make friends with the fairies

Before you could count three, there was a new pointed cap sitting on Kasperl's head. It was as like his old one **as two peas in a pod.**

"Wonderful!", said Seppel. "If I hadn't seen Hotzenplotz throw your old cap into the fire with my own eyes, I'd never believe that this was a new one. Now, come on."

"All right", said Kasperl. "I'm coming now."

Carrying the birdcage between them, and whistling cheerfully, they walked towards home.

"How happy I feel!", said Kasperl after a while.

"So do I!", said Seppel. "Grandmother will be happy too."

"Grandmother!", Kasperl suddenly stopped. "Oh, good gracious me, Seppel!"

"What's the matter? Why have you stopped?"

"I've thought of something. We almost forgot the most important thing of all!"

"The most important thing of all ...?"

"Yes", said Kasperl. "Grandmother's coffee mill!"

"Oh dear!", groaned Seppel, putting his hands to his head. "You're quite right, Kasperl! We must have Grandmother's coffee mill – it's no good going home without it. Well, let's go back to the robber's cave."

"Wait a minute!", said Kasperl. "I know a trick worth two of that!"

He turned his wishing ring for the second time.

"I wish for Grandmother's coffee mill back", he said.

There was a **thud** – and Grandmother's coffee mill was lying in the grass at his feet.

"Goodness!", cried Seppel. "That was quick work. Is it all right?"

He picked it up and tried it.

The coffee mill was working all right; when he turned the handle it played "Nuts in May". And wonder of wonders – it played "Nuts in May" as a duet.

"A duet!", gasped Seppel. "How lovely! Grandmother will like it, too. How did it happen? Can you explain it?"

Kasperl agreed that it was very odd.

"Perhaps the fairy Amaryllis had something to do with it?", he suggested.

"Oh yes, of course!", said Seppel. "She wanted to give us all a nice surprise! Now, what about the third wish?"

"Can't you guess what the third wish is for?", asked Kasperl. "*I* know what to do with it."

button: Knopf – **to talk a mile a minute:** lang und breit erzählen – **brute:** Grobian, Haderlump – **behind bars:** hinter Schloss und Riegel – **to be as like as two peas in a pod:** sich wie ein Ei dem anderen gleichen – **thud:** Plumps

A Great Day for Sergeant Dimplemoser

Grandmother was worried to death.

She had no idea what could be keeping Kasperl and Seppel all this time.

The day before, Grandmother had been to the police station three times to see Sergeant Dimplemoser. Now she was off to try once more.

She hoped Sergeant Dimplemoser would have some good news at last.

"Have you found out anything about Kasperl and Seppel, Sergeant?", she asked.

"No, I'm afraid not", said Sergeant Dimplemoser. He was sitting at the desk eating his breakfast.

"You haven't?", asked Grandmother, beginning to cry.

"No", repeated the sergeant. "I'm sorry, but that's all I can tell you, Grandmother. I've found no trace of either of them."

"No trace at all?"

The sergeant shrugged his shoulders.

"The only **clue** we *have* found is that handcart over there in the corner. Do you know it?"

"Yes", sobbed Grandmother. "Kasperl and Seppel took it out with them yesterday morning. Where did you find it?"

"It was lying upside down in the ditch beside the road. We turned it right way up again."

"And now what?", asked Grandmother.

"Mmph – now what?", muttered Sergeant Dimplemoser.

He frowned heavily as he thought the problem over. Then he suddenly banged the desk top. The breakfast things tinkled and clattered.

"Grandmother!", he cried. "I have an idea! Do you know what we'll do? We'll have the **town crier** make a public proclamation about them!"

"Do you think that will help?", asked Grandmother.

"We'll have to wait and see. It can't do any harm, anyway."

Sergeant Dimplemoser pushed his breakfast things aside. He took a big sheet of paper out of the drawer of his desk, dipped his pen into the ink and began to write:

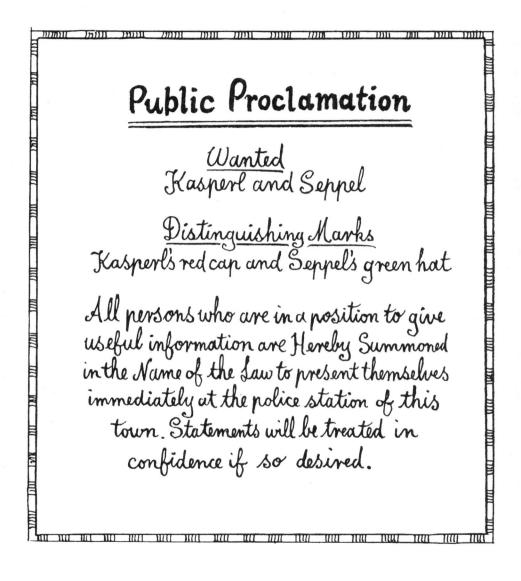

Public Proclamation

Wanted
Kasperl and Seppel

Distinguishing Marks
Kasperl's red cap and Seppel's green hat

All persons who are in a position to give useful information are Hereby Summoned in the Name of the Law to present themselves immediately at the police station of this town. Statements will be treated in confidence if so desired.

"There!", said Sergeant Dimplemoser with satisfaction. "All it needs now is my signature ..."

He was just about to put his usual flourishing signature at the bottom of the paper. But it turned into a huge **blot**. For just at the **crucial** moment, the door flew open and in rushed Kasperl and Seppel.

"Oh!", cried Grandmother. She nearly fainted again, for joy this time.

"Hello!", shouted Kasperl and Seppel. "Here we are!"

Grandmother hugged them, laughing and crying at the same time.

"How glad I am to see you again!", she said. "I've been so worried. Is it really you? I can hardly believe it! Isn't this a wonderful surprise, Sergeant?"

Sergeant Dimplemoser had come around to the other side of the desk. He was looking very cross and official.

"I must say, this is a bit too much!", he said. "Now I've gone and wasted a whole sheet of paper. Couldn't you have come here sooner?"

"I'm afraid not, Sergeant", said Kasperl. "But never mind, we've brought you a present."

"What is it?", asked Sergeant Dimplemoser.

"We've brought you the robber Hotzenplotz!", said Kasperl.

"**Snakes alive!**", cried the sergeant in amazement. "Where is he?"

"Here he is", said Kasperl.

He walked up to the desk and put down the birdcage.

114

At this, Sergeant Dimplemoser flew into a rage.

"What?", he cried. "What's all this? What do you mean by it? Do you think I'm **putting up** with this? I'm an officer of the law. Play your silly tricks on anyone you like, as long as it's not me. People who play tricks on me get sent to prison."

"All right, Sergeant, all right", said Kasperl. And he turned the wishing ring on his finger.

"I wish for the cuckoo in the cage to turn back into the robber Hotzenplotz", he said.

At once the third and last wish was granted. The robber Hotzenplotz stood where the cuckoo had been. He was standing in the middle of Sergeant Dimplemoser's desk, wearing his warm dressing gown. He had no shoes on, and he had the birdcage over his head.

"Hey, you!", shouted Sergeant Dimplemoser. "Get off my desk! What do you mean by climbing up there? How did you get here all of a sudden – and who are you, anyway?"

"Just a minute, Sergeant!", said Kasperl. "This is the robber Hotzenplotz. Aren't you going to arrest him?"

It didn't make sense to Sergeant Dimplemoser.

"This is supposed to be the robber Hotzenplotz, is it?", he cried. "Nonsense! Whoever saw a robber in stocking feet!"

"Yes, he is!", said Grandmother. "I recognize him – he really is the robber Hotzenplotz. You must –"

But the robber Hotzenplotz interrupted her. "Out of the way there!", he shouted.

He leaped off the desk and ran past Sergeant Dimplemoser to the open window. He plunged through head first, hoping to escape. But Seppel grabbed his feet, and Kasperl promptly let down the iron shutter. Crash! The robber Hotzenplotz was trapped.

He struggled like a fish out of water.

"Seppel, see that he stays quiet!", said Kasperl. He ran out into the garden with Sergeant Dimplemoser.

Hotzenplotz's head and the top part of his body were hanging out of the window. He was waving his arms as if he were learning to swim.

"Help! I can't breathe. I'm finished!", he gasped. „How long is this going on?"

"That depends", said Kasperl. "If you'll only keep still we'll have you out in a moment."

"All right then!", panted Hotzenplotz. He realized that it was all up now.

He stopped **threshing about** and let Sergeant Dimplemoser bind his hands behind his back. Then Seppel raised the shutter a little way.

Sergeant Dimplemoser and Kasperl pulled the robber Hotzenplotz out of the window. The old scoundrel landed heavily in the garden like a sack of potatoes.

"There", grunted Sergeant Dimplemoser with satisfaction. "Now we've got you. Off we go now. I must put you safely under lock and key."

The robber Hotzenplotz got up with difficulty. "Can't you take this cage off my head?", he asked.

"No", said Sergeant Dimplemoser. "The cage stays put!"

He drew his sword. But before marching Hotzenplotz off, he hurriedly thanked Kasperl and Seppel for their help.

"I'll see that you get a reward from the **Mayor** tomorrow", Sergeant Dimplemoser finished. "Then you must tell me all about it. I'll have to put it all down in the evidence, you see. Till tomorrow goodbye!"

Sergeant Dimplemoser led the robber Hotzenplotz three times around the town. The people came running out of their houses to stare. They were glad the robber was caught at last.

"What will happen to him now?", they all asked.

"First I shall put him behind bars", said the sergeant.

"And then what?

"Then we'll **have the law on** him."

clue: Anhaltspunkt – **town crier**: Gemeindediener – **blot**: Klecks – **crucial**: entscheidend – **snakes alive!**: Sapperlot! – **to put up with**: sich gefallen lassen – **to thresh about**: dreschen, wüten – **Mayor**: Bürgermeister – **to have the law on s.b.**: jmd. den Prozess machen

Coffee and Plum Pie

Kasperl and Seppel sat in Grandmother's sittingroom beaming with pleasure. How good it was to be home at last! It was hard to realize that only three days had passed since the last time they all sat here together.

Grandmother was beaming, too. She quickly **laid the table**. Then she ran out of the kitchen and brought in a big plum pie. She put a bowl of whipped cream on the table as well.

"Why, Grandmother!", said Kasperl in surprise. "It's not Sunday today, is it?"

"Of course it is", said Grandmother. "It may be Wednesday in other people's houses, but it's Sunday here."

She looked in the mirror and set her cap straight. Then she hurried to the door.

"Are you going out?", asked Kasperl.

"Just to borrow a coffee mill. I can't manage without one."

"No", said Kasperl with a grin, "of course you can't. There you are!"

He produced the coffee mill and put it on the table. Then he waited to hear what Grandmother would say.

At first Grandmother could say nothing at all.

She picked up the coffee mill and began to turn the handle. The coffee mill played "Nuts in May" as a duet.

Kasperl and Seppel kept perfectly quiet.

"Oh!", said Grandmother at last. "How lovely! Do you know how I feel?"

"How do you feel?"

"I feel as if it were my birthday and Christmas both at once! And now I'll make the coffee."

Grandmother made the nicest pot of coffee she had ever made in her life. When the pot was standing on the table and all the cups were full, Kasperl and Seppel had to tell their story.

"You make my hair **stand on end!**", said Grandmother, shaking her head. "You really make my hair stand on end!", she repeated over and over again.

Now and then she took a **sip** from her coffee cup. Kasperl and Seppel had plum pie with whipped cream. They ate plum pie until they had stomach ache, and they were so happy that they wouldn't have changed places with anyone, not even the Emperor of Constantinople.

to lay the table: den Tisch decken – **to stand on end:** zu Berge stehen – **sip:** Schlückchen

Contents

The Man With Seven Knives 5

A Helping Hand for the Police 10

Caution – Gold! 16

A Piece of Bad Luck 21

Heavily Disguised 27

A Pistol Full of Pepper 32

A Gloomy Outlook 36

Petrosilius Zackleman 41

An Adventure in the Dark 49

As Stupid as Possible 55

Poor Seppel! 60

Three Doors in the Cellar 65

The Mysterious Toad 71

The Open Heath 76

"The Owner of the Hat" 80

A Magician of his Word 85

The End of Petrosilius Zackleman 92

A Fairy Lady 98

A Wishing Ring 104

A Great Day for Sergeant Dimplemoser 111

Coffee and Plum Pie 120

Dieses Buch wurde in folgende Fremdsprachen übersetzt:
Afrikaans, Amerikanisch, Chinesisch, Dänisch, Englisch, Estnisch, Finnisch,
Französisch, Gälisch/Kymrisch, Griechisch, Holländisch, Italienisch,
Japanisch, Katalanisch, Koreanisch, Ladinisch, Litauisch, Norwegisch,
Polnisch, Portugiesisch, Rumänisch, Russisch, Schwedisch, Serbokroatisch,
Slowenisch, Spanisch, Surselvisch, Türkisch, Ukrainisch.

Preußler, Otfried:
The Robber Hotzenplotz
Aus dem Deutschen von Anthea Bell
ISBN 3 522 17610 3

Gesamtausstattung: F.J. Tripp
Einbandtypografie: Michael Kimmerle
Satz: KCS GmbH in Buchholz/Hamburg
Reproduktion: immedia 23 in Stuttgart
Druck und Bindung: Friedrich Pustet in Regensburg
© 2003 by Thienemann Verlag
(Thienemann Verlag GmbH), Stuttgart/Wien
Printed in Germany. Alle Rechte vorbehalten.
7 6 5 4 3* 04 05 06 07

Thienemann im Internet: www.thienemann.de

Otfried Preußler im Internet: www.preussler.de